Buzz and Bingo in the Fairytale Forest

"Hello, I'm Buzz and this is Bingo!"

"Woof!"

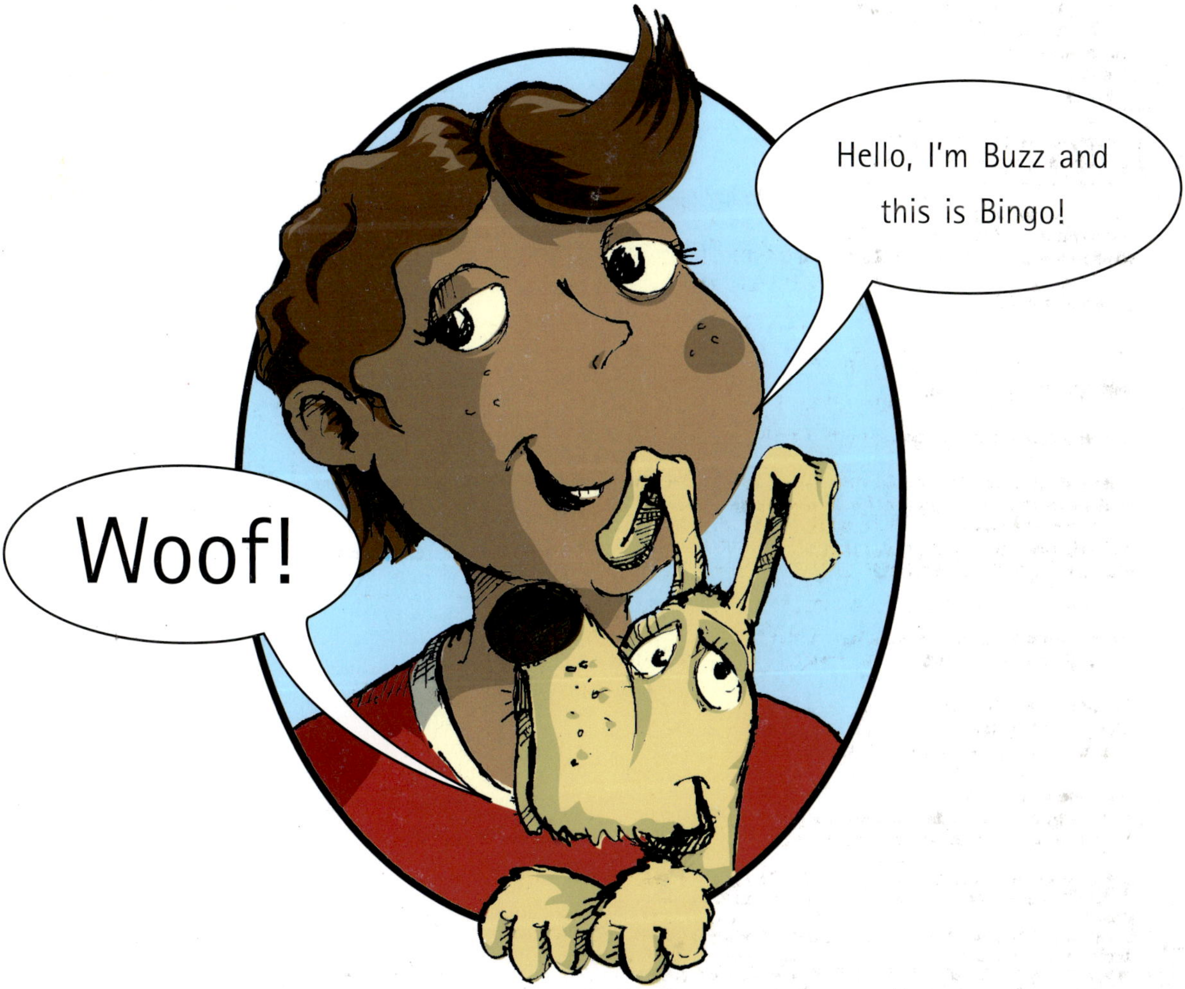

Written by Alan Durant
Illustrated by Sholto Walker

Chapter One

Once upon a time, Buzz and Bingo walked into a dark forest and met an old woman.

"Good morning," said Buzz.

"It's not good for me, young sir," groaned the old woman. "I have a present for a kind and beautiful girl who lives in this forest, but I can't find her. I don't know what to do."

Buzz smiled. "Don't be sad," he said. "Bingo and I will find her for you."

"Oh, thank you, sir," said the old woman. "Please give her this gift from me."

A little further on, Buzz and Bingo met a prince who was holding a glass slipper.

"Good morning, sir," said Buzz. "I wonder if you can help me? I'm looking for a beautiful girl who lives in this forest."

"So am I," the prince sighed. "I danced with her last night at the palace ball. When the clock struck midnight, she fled, leaving behind only this slipper. I must find her again. I'm Charming by the way."
Buzz smiled. "I'm sure you are," he said.
"No, that's my name," said the prince, "Prince Charming."
"Well, Prince Charming, why don't you come with us? We'll search together," said Buzz.

They had not gone far when they met a large wolf with an empty basket.

"Good morning, Mr Wolf," said Buzz. "We're looking for a beautiful girl who lives in the forest."

"Why, so am I!" exclaimed the wolf, showing a row of huge, sharp teeth. "She's perfectly delicious."

"Delicious?" Buzz asked.

"I mean delightful," the wolf corrected himself. "She left her basket in the woods and I wish to return it to her."

"I see," said Buzz. "Well, perhaps you'd like to join our search."
"Oh, so kind," purred the wolf.
Bingo growled.

Chapter Two

Buzz, Bingo, Prince Charming and Mr Wolf walked on through the forest. They met …

… a boy with some magical beans …

… a frog prince …

… a puss in boots …

8

... a brother and sister lost in the woods ...

... and a tiny girl no bigger than Buzz's thumb ...

... but none of them knew where the beautiful girl lived.

Suddenly they heard the sound of singing.
It grew louder and louder and louder.
Soon one, two, three, four, five, six, seven little men appeared.
They were carrying sacks and tools.

"Good day, gentlemen," said Buzz.
"We're looking for a beautiful girl who lives in the forest.
Can you help us?"

"Who wants to know?" asked the first little man, grumpily.
Buzz smiled. "My name's Buzz," he said.
"This is Prince Charming. And this is Mr Wolf."
"Woof!" barked Bingo.
"Oh, and my dog Bingo," Buzz added.
"I have a gift for the girl."
"I want to marry her," sighed the prince.
"I want to eat her," growled the wolf.
"Meet her, I mean," he quickly corrected himself.

The little men talked among themselves for a moment or two. "Come with us," said the little man at last.

Buzz, Bingo, Prince Charming and Mr Wolf followed the seven little men through the forest.

Chapter Three

Soon they came to a small cottage.
The first little man knocked at the door.
"We're home!" he called.

A moment later, the door opened. There stood the most beautiful girl that any of them had ever seen.

"Snow White," said the little man.
"Cinderella," sighed the prince.
"Little Red Riding Hood," slurped the wolf.
"Woof!" said Bingo.

Buzz gave Snow White the gift.
"Oh, how nice," she said. It was a beautiful, red apple.
But she was looking at Prince Charming.
It was love at first sight.
"Please try on this slipper," said the prince, adoringly.
"Happily," Snow White replied.

But the slipper didn't quite fit.

"Oh well, who cares?" shrugged Prince Charming. He tossed the slipper out of the window. He got down on one knee and said, "Will you marry me?"

"Of course," said Snow White and she kissed the prince.

Meanwhile, the wolf put the beautiful, red apple in his basket. He sneaked away, licking his lips, and back in the forest, he took a huge bite.

On their way home, Buzz and Bingo met the old woman again. She was looking into a mirror. "We found the beautiful girl and gave her your gift," said Buzz.

The old woman cackled. "And did she eat it?" she asked. "Well, no," Buzz said. "Actually, a wolf took it."

"A wolf!" shrieked the old woman. She flew into a rage and smashed the mirror. "But I must be the fairest of them all," she screamed. "I think it's time we went home, Bingo," said Buzz.

But Bingo was already half way home.
He'd had quite enough of fairy-tale adventures.
He wanted to live happily ever after!

Ideas for guided reading

Learning objectives: To tell real and imagined stories using the conventions of familiar story language, to predict story endings, to discuss and compare story themes, to identify and describe characters expressing own views, to understand the use of antonyms

Interest words: charming, beautiful, delightful, fairest

Curriculum links: Citizenship: People who help us (Keeping ourselves safe)

Word count: 772

Resources: whiteboard, pens, paper

Getting started

This book can be read over two sessions.

- Introduce the book to the children, and discuss the cover and blurb. Have they read about these two characters before? (They may have read the Purple level book *Buzz and Bingo in the Monster Maze*.)
- Ask the children to scan through book up to p21. Can they identify any of the other characters from picture cues? Prompt them to look for evidence, e.g. the mirror and the apple suggest the wicked stepmother from 'Snow White'. Discuss what all the other characters have in common – they are all from fairy tales. Which are they from?
- Choose one character and model how to tell their original story briefly.
- Ask the children, in pairs, to pick a character and retell their story, using the opening phrase 'Once upon a time...'

Reading and responding

- Ask the children to read the story silently and independently, until p21.
- Remind children of strategies they can use for unfamiliar words, including making connections with previous stories. Listen to each child read aloud separately and observe, prompt and praise as they read for meaning.
- Prompts include 'How would you say these words if you were that character', stressing understanding of character traits, 'You sounded just like the big bad wolf then...'
- Children not reading to teacher carry on reading silently and check their predictions.
- When the children are all finished, look at pp22–23 and ask them to recap what happens at each point of the forest marked by a picture.